Rennell Rodd

The Violet Crown

And Songs of England

Rennell Rodd

The Violet Crown
And Songs of England

ISBN/EAN: 9783744769136

Printed in Europe, USA, Canada, Australia, Japan

Cover: Foto ©Andreas Hilbeck / pixelio.de

More available books at **www.hansebooks.com**

THE VIOLET CROWN

AND

SONGS OF ENGLAND

BY

RENNELL RODD

AUTHOR OF "FEDA," "THE UNKNOWN MADONNA," ETC.

WITH A FRONTISPIECE

BY

THE MARCHIONESS OF GRANBY

LONDON

DAVID STOTT, 370, OXFORD STREET, W

MDCCCXCI.

Of the following poems, six have already appeared in *Murray's Magazine,* three in *Harper's Monthly,* and one in *Macmillan's Magazine,* to the respective Editors of which I here make my acknowledgments for the permission to reprint them.

R. R.

CONTENTS.

The Violet Crown.

CONTENTS.

Songs of England.

Miscellaneous Poems.

THE VIOLET CROWN.

———

À

MADAME MARY BAKHMÉTEFF

(SOUVENIR DU PENTÉLIQUE).

1889.

THE VIOLET CROWN.

THE VIOLET CROWN.

WHEREFORE the " city of the violet crown " ?
One asked me, as the April sun went down
Behind the shadows of the Persian's mound,
The fretted crags of Salamis.

         " Look round,
And see the question answered ! "

              For we were
Upon the summit of that battled square,
The rock of ruin, in whose fallen shrine
The world still worships what it deems divine,
The maiden fane, that yet may boast the birth
Of half the immortalities of earth.

                               B

The last rays light the portal, a gold wave
Runs up the columns to the architetrave,
Lingers about the gable and is gone :—
Parnes, Hymettus, and Pentelicon
Show shadowy violet in the after-rose,
Cithæron's ridge and all the islands close
The mountain ring, like sapphires o'er the sea
And from this circle's heart ætherially
Springs the white altar of the land's renown,
A marble lily in a violet crown.

And fairer crown had never queen than this
That girds thee round, far-famed Acropolis !
So of these isles, these mountains, and this sea,
I wove a crown of song to dedicate to thee.

ATHENS, 1890.

THITHER.

BEYOND Albania's headlands high,
The misted sun rose, struggled free,
Outblanched the roses of the sky,
And flashed upon an opal sea;
Then, from their mythos-world of night,
The poet's islands swam in sight—
That link between the east and west,
Phæacia's pleasant land of rest;
The land of men that loved the oar,
Which, in the morning light of yore,
Poseidon to his kinsfolk gave,
And made them masters of the wave;
And many an isle less known to fame,
Like floating leaves and flowers came;
And many a shore by sea-nymphs ranged,
Ere gods and men became estranged;
Till, through the hush of afternoon,
We sailed between the sun and moon,

By Leucas and the lovers' leap,

Where still the amorous breezes weep

The echoes of a Lesbian air

And Sappho's purple-shadowed hair ;

Then last, as bleak and barren still,

His home, the man of iron will,

Of many a wile and many a part,

Odysseus, of the stubborn heart,

Which never, never since he fared

On that mysterious voyage, dared

Explore the untried western deep,

Has broken through her trance of sleep.

The sunset flushed her capes and caves,

And lingered on the wine-red waves ;

Till late beyond our eastward prow

The moonlight blanched a mountain brow,

And shadows of the violet seas

Closed o'er the isles Echinades.

Then, as it were a giant bay,

The hills closed in on either hand,

To north the rough Ætolia lay

And on the south was Pelops' land.

1889.

THE KEYNOTE.

A CYPRESS dark against the blue,
That deepens up to such a hue
As never painter dared and drew ;

A marble shaft that stands alone
Above a wreck of sculptured stone
With gray-green aloes overgrown ;

A hill-side scored with hollow veins
Through age-long wash of autumn rains,
As purple as with vintage stains ;

And rocks that while the hours run
Show all the jewels, one by one,
For pastime of the summer sun ;

A crescent sail upon the sea,
So calm and fair and ripple-free,
You wonder storms can ever be ;

A shore with deep indented bays,
And o'er the gleaming waterways
A glimpse of islands in the haze ;

A face bronzed dark to red and gold,
With mountain eyes that seem to hold
The freshness of the world of old ;

A shepherd's crook, a coat of fleece,
A grazing flock ;—the sense of peace,
The long sweet silence,—this is Greece !

1890.

MISOLONGHI.

The rosy dawn broke from her ocean bed—
A sailor pointed to the north, and said
The one word, " Misolonghi!"   Lifted high,
Between the mists of water and of sky,
In the mirage of sunrise, there it lay,
The heart of Hellas in her darkest day.

And there and then, across that morning sea,
The eager heart went throbbing back to thee,
For here, dead poet of my dreams of youth,
Thy long denial learned the one hard truth.

Oft with thee since, my poet, where the steep
Of Sunium sees red evening dye the deep,
Where broad Eurotas cleaves the garden lands
That knew no walls but Spartan hearts and hands,
Where snowy-crested into cloudless skies
The two throne-mountains of the muses rise ;

Mount up, oh poet, still they seem to say,

Pathless and lonely winds the starward way,

Look never back, thou hast thy song to sing,

Thy life is winter, so thy death be spring.

Oft with thee after, when the sun went down

Behind Morea, through the violet crown,

Seen from the broken temples, when the ray

Transforms Hymettus from noon's silver grey

To one rose jewel, when the islands be

Like broken sapphires on a milky sea,

And still thy mute voice echoes near, but most

A moment later when the light is lost,

And Athens sobers in the afterglow

Of such a spiritual twilight as I know

No other spot of sea and earth can show ;

Thou art grown one with these things, and thy fame

Links a new memory to each sacred name.

Oh formed for loving, and condemned by fate,

By some obstruction of the heart, to hate,

Cursed with the spirit of an evil doubt,

That would not open when love knocked without.

Doomed to rebellion, and untimely born,
To mar high music with the note of scorn,
Appealing still against thyself in song,
How I had loved thee, erring, proud, and strong !

Yet, let me think here by these haunted seas,
Too fair to need their dower of memories ;
Here, where the whisperings of spring-tide eve
Bring kinship with the infinite, and weave
Bright rosaries of stars, where never fails
Incense of thyme, and hymn of nightingales,
That oft the beauty of this fair world stole
Across the tumult of thy lonely soul,
Till the ice thawed, and the storm broke in spray,
The cold heart warmed, and knew the better way,
To see some hope in human things, to crave
That late remorse of love men lavished on thy grave.

AN ATTIC NIGHT.

ABOVE Hymettus' long dark sundering ridge—
Not cold and chaste as in my own far world,
But pale for passion and yet warm with love—
Midsummer's moon bends earthward, and the stars
Pale at her advent ; through the cypress tops
A silent shiver of delight runs o'er,
And dreaming earth grows open-eyed once more.

These hill-side aloes pierce the sapphire night
Like some great battle struck into a trance
With all its sword-blades lifted, and above
An ivory stair climbs up the silver rocks
Through roofless columns of a marble gate ;
This is the rock of Athens, reared sublime,
Crowned with quick stars above the night of time.

Enter the door of silence ! Far away
The thousand twinkling little lights recede,

And stars grow nearer, while the flitting owls
Repeat unseen the same shrill note in sound,
The nomad bells of flocks that move by night
Come from the distance :—thou art all alone
With shadows haunting a dead world of stone,

Lo with a mystic radiance round its scars,
Hardly a ruin in this healing light,
The fairest pile that ever human hearts
Built to enshrine their young ideal mood !
The moon is on one side the colonnade,
Steals through its rent of battle, seeks in vain
The sister goddess in her fallen fane.

Alas for dead ideals, and alas
Immortal moods are bounded by a day !
Once only here such throbbing life upburst
To the full at every issue, snatched the fire
Quick from the life springs, dared and overcame
While still the childhood of the heart was free ;
There was but once one Athens, or could be !

Here wrought the strong creator, and he laid
The marble on the limestone, in the crag
Morticed and sure foundations, line to line
And arc to arc repeating, as it grew ;
Veiling the secret of its strength in grace,
Till like a marble flower in blue Greek air
Perfect it rose, an afterworld's despair.

And here man made his most divine appeal
To the eternal in the heart of man,
The mute appeal of beauty, crying still
Dimly across the ages that are dumb.
And lo ! it lies a ruin, and the owls
Dwell in the splintered cornice, and the moon
Blanches the broken discords into tune.

Come from the ruin, this despairing note
Steals like a siren music on the soul
And the sweet way of sadness lures ; come forth !
For now the moon has mounted, and yon sea
Is all a fire of jewels,—far away
To dim Ægina misty in the west
She takes the benediction on her breast.

And all the mountains are a wonder world
Of untried promise, and the larger stars
Burn steadfast still, and from the south there comes
A breath like odours blown from Paradise
Scented and cool and soothing ; so we turn
From man's supremest to God's every day,
And dimly feel our solace lies that way.

Burn on bright stars ! gleam through the night
 white sea !
If I have loved the living world of men,
Their hopes and dreams the labour of their hands,
And trusted much and, doubting, trusted still,
Yet nature was my mother and my guide,
And ever nearest, and when all else failed,
Her arms were open still and her great love prevailed.

 1890.

GENIUS LOCI.

Scent of the pine-tree and breath of the rose
Hang in the wake of the wind as it blows :

Songs in the coppice, and mingled with these
The murmur of insects from under the trees :

The sun's in the heaven, the lark's on the wing,
The fulness of summer grows out of the spring.

All these are round me, and you by my side,
You in the glory of youth at its pride ;

Cheeks that are roses, a rose for a mouth,
The wonderful lustre of eyes of the south ;

Soothe me with music, and sing to me, sing,
Conjure me back to the passion of spring !

The sun on the rose, and the wind in the tree,
Are whispering love as you whisper to me ;

The wind on the tree, and the sun on the rose,
Will scourge them and scorch them when summer-
　　time goes ;

Dreams for the dreamer, and saws for the sage,
There is time to grow wise in the winter of age !

Therefore, sweet Pagan, whose name is a song,
Love me as long as the summer is long !

　　1889.

ILISSUS' BANK.

A PLANE-TREE by Ilissus' bed,
A bank of shade to prop the head,
With scanty grass, and frequent stone—
A summer noon to dream alone.

The hand of change has touched the scene,
No more are meads of pleasant green ;
The thin few trees have much ado
To leaf a little, and renew
The ravage of the autumn suns
By channels where no water runs.
But as of old the tettix trills,
The bee booms past to heather hills,
And in the mountain gulleys deep
The blue noon shadows lie asleep.

Yet not alone—for by the stream
Were two that walked the path of dream ;

The one, who seemed the type and flower
Of Athens in her golden hour,
When youth and strength were tuned to grace ;
And one, the plain, familiar face—
The man that I would rather meet
Some evening in the tripod-street,
With gait uncouth and dome-shaped brow,
Than all the world of then or now :
The thick lips parted, and the hands
Close clasped behind his back, he stands,
With head thrust out, and starting eyes
That bear the glare of noonday skies.

And first the younger had his say,
That presence like a fresh spring day,
An eloquent impulsive strain,
While I sat quiet by the plane.

Then might he hear who listened well
The tale I heard the elder tell :
Of love's ideal, which is truth,
The fluttering of the soul of youth

C

Aspiring still to seek above
That far-off, dim-remembered love,
Till, gazing up to heavenly things,
It finds at last the long-lost wings.

The noon goes by, the even rose
Fades up Hymettus' side and goes,
A wind comes shoreward from the sea,
And wakes a rustle in the tree,
The shadows fall, and even so
The dream is done ; yet, ere I go,
I, too, may pray the prayer he prayed
To Pan and whatso Dryad maid
Possessed the soul of summer trees
And shed sweet influence over these,
If not to such, as best I know
The prayer he made long years ago,
For beauty in the inward soul—
The path is changed but not the goal.

1890.

THERMOPYLÆ.

THIS is the place;—the mountain bay
   Is wild, and stern, and grand,
As when the Lion held the way
   That barred his mother-land.
Long years and change and earthquake shock
   Have wrought upon the scene,
Where once the sea waves lapped the rock
   Are meadow lands grown green;
But Oeta still looms vast and grey
   To hide the setting sun,
And still the mountains bar the way,
   And every way but one:
The sulphur springs still fume and flow
   Along the rough hill-side,
And far-off Othrys veiled in snow
   Sees where the Spartan died.

There is a spirit haunts the place
   Where mighty deeds were dared,

Though time and change have left no trace,
　　And not a grave be spared :
And climbing up the grassy hill
　　Where Sparta's lion stood ;
The heart still answers to the thrill,
　　That marks the hero mood.

And as I read the page again,
　　That quickens from the dust
The tale of those three hundred men
　　Who died to keep their trust,
I knew the fire was not yet lost
　　That nerved my younger age :—
The shadow of an eagle crossed,
　　And fell along my page !

SUNSET IN ÆGINA.

THE light that is on sea and sky
   This April eve of earth
Would touch the saddest heart to mirth,
   Or reconcile the lightest mood
     To kinship with a sigh :—
The little cloud-flakes, evening's own,
   Red with the dead day's blood,
Seem scattered rose leaves overblown
   Upon a windless mere ;
The sapphire mountains fret the gold,
   These more than mountains here—
The dream-hills of the songs of old—
   Cut luminous and clear :
The glow is on the April green,
And every outline softly keen
   Stands out against the sunset sheen.
The world is washed in such a flood of air
   So rosy and so freshly fair,

As though if God in heaven saw meet
  To sweep all stains away,
And leave earth pure and virgin-sweet
  As on creation-day.

Oh ship, with sails against the sun,
  Dark on the amber deep,
Thou wilt not make beyond the west
A better island of the blest !

  The splendid day was past and done,
    The day we could not keep,
  The purple died along the slope,
    The moon blanched in the blue,
  And steadfast like a good man's hope
    The star of evening grew.

ÆGINA, 1890.

DELOS.

WE came to an isle of flowers
    That lay in a trance of sleep,
In a world forgotten of ours,
    Far out on a sapphire deep.

Dwellers were none on the island,
    And far as the eye could see
From the shore to the central highland
    Was never a bush nor tree.

Long, long had her fields lain fallow,
    And the drought had dried her rills,
But the vetch and the gourd and mallow
    Ran riot on all her hills.

The length of her shoreward level,
    High bank and terrace and quay,
Were red with a scarlet revel
    Of poppies down to the sea;

Each bloom pressed close on its fellow,
   The marigolds peeped between,
Till the scarlet and the yellow
   Had hidden the under-green.

Was it here, that heart of a nation,
   That first of the fanes of old !
This garden of desolation,
   This ruin of red, of gold?

High up from the rock-cleft hollow,
   Roofed over of Titan hands;
The cradle of dead Apollo
   Still looks to his silent lands.

The sacred lake lies solemn,
   In a havoc of fallen shrines;
Where the shaft of each broken column
   Is tangled about with vines.

It lives in the dreams which haunt it,
   This isle of the Sun-god's birth,
It lives in the songs which vaunt it
   The holiest earth on earth.

But the shrines without note or number
  Lie wrecked on a barren shore,
And the dead ideals slumber
  For ever and evermore.

So Spring in her pride of pity
  Had hidden the marble wraith,
And shed on the holy city
  The flower of sleep and death.

IN ARCADIA.

To L. S.

I THINK we shall keep for ever in the heart of us, you
    and I,
That first Arcadian evening, till the day we come to die.

We had crossed from the rugged border, through the
    fierce Messenian hills,
And we came to the oak-wood pastures, to a ripple of
    mountain rills.

The late noon waned to the eventide and the
    gathering in of flocks,
The shepherd called with his uncouth cries to the
    goats far up in the rocks ;

While the kids leaped down with their startled eyes,
    and paused for a drink at the spring,
As he strode along in his kilted pride, with the gait of
    a mountain king.

The steep hills sloped to a narrow vale through
willow and oak and pear,
To the gold-green sage on the further side, and the
thyme that hung in the air ;
.

The corn-plots waved in the hollow, and the planes
were marvellous green,
Where the young nymph-haunted Neda was a luminous
thread between.

The day went over the westward ridge too soon in
the mountain world,
And the thousand frail sun-wearied convolvulus bells
were furled.

A turtle cooed on the farther side, and the scented air
of the vale
Was quick with tremulous throbbing of the song of
the nightingale.

A mist rose up from the waters and the stream-nymph
veiled her charms,
Where the mountain clasped her closest in the grasp
of his purple arms.

It was red gold over the western peaks and pale gold
  over the sky,
It was middle May in the full moon time, and the
  land was Arcady!

And the scent of the thyme and the song of the bird
  drew a calm down over the breast,
The stream ran by with a soothing voice, and the
  note of it all was rest.

Ah, well with you, happy valleys, where the roar of
  the world is still,
Where the brain may pause in the battle of life, and
  the eyes may drink their fill!

And well with you, fair green isles, in your girdle of
  surf apart,
With never a rumour of march and change, Avalons
  of the weary heart!

The sunset over those gilded hills was more than an
  earthly name,
The moon was brighter than glory, the stars seemed
  better than fame.

And we, we shall keep I know in the heart of us, you
    and I,
That first Arcadian evening till the day we come to
    die.

    DRAGOI, 1890.

THE SIREN SONG.

I HEARD it in the happy isles
Blown down the dying day,
The summer song whose lilt beguiles
The wanderer to stay :

It followed in the shorewind's breath,
The magic still was strong,
Although the note of change and death
Has touched the Sirens' song.

They do not lure to new delights
Beyond what life has known,
To happy days and happy nights
In summer's slumber-zone ;

But only, " who will rest awhile
From riot and from ruth,
Forget in such a sunny smile
The brazen eyes of truth !

"Come hither, hither, come and dream
    Of years dead long ago,
    Until the earth and ocean seem
    The world that poets know.

"Come back and dwell with hopes long dead
    And what will never be !
    Avert thine eyes and turn thine head
    From the world's way oversea !

"For here are drowsy dreams to cheat
    The eyes that else would weep,
    And inland seas to bathe the feet,
    And quiet vales for sleep."

But deadly is the Sirens' song
    As ever in the ears,
    And ropes of faith must bind him strong
    Who bides it when he hears.

For some have hearkened, lain them down
    And drunk a deadly thing,
    And soon the storms of winter drown
    The hollow hope of spring.

Pass, phantom music, pass away !
The purple isles grow dim ;
The glamour of the dying day
Fades on the ocean's rim.

Enchantress of the mossy caves
Sleep by thy drowsy streams !
The cradle of the rocking waves
Is worth a world of dreams !

Oh living love, my happy hills
Be wheresoe'er thou art !
There is no help for human ills
But in the human heart ;

So be the haven near or far,
Blow winds and freshen sea,
The morrow's hope, the morning star,
The living world for me !

1889.

TÆNARON.

Nè dolcezza di figlio, nè la piéta
 Del vecchio padre, nè il debito amore
Lo qual dovea Penelope far lieta,
 Vincer potero dentro a me l'ardore
Ch'io ebbi a divenir del mondo esperto,
 E degli vizj umani, e del valore.

Inferno, XXVI.

THE sun sank slowly through the purple waves,
   Flashed yet a moment on bluff Matapan,
   While up the crest a rosy glamour ran,
And shadows deepened in the gaps and caves.

I came that evening to a little creek,
   After long travel through a stone-cursed land,
   Rock only, rock above, on either hand—
A barren wilderness, and what to seek?

A race as wild as nature where they dwell
   Nested in towers on the mountain crown,
   Blood in their passions, murder their renown
An ancient race, since Lacedæmon fell

D

And the war-flutes shrilled no longer, and strange folk
　　With alien voices thronged the land, and drank
　　From sacred fountains, Moslem, Sclave, or Frank
These stubborn mountains never felt their yoke

It was full summer in the Southern May,
　　And all day long I rode among the rocks,
　　Stumbled and clattered through the marble blocks,
Till even stayed me by a little bay,

Hid in the hollow of the sea-cliff's arm,
　　Half shelving shore and half a rock-wall sheer
　　Above whose rim one dim star rose to peer;—
The silence wrought upon me like a charm.

A summer peace lay on the sapphire deep,
　　Only close by a few late ripples played
　　O'er hues of coral, ambergris, and jade,
And darker madders where the oar-weeds sleep.

A little bark that dared not venture nigh
　　Showed through the sea-cliff's shadow; but no tree,
　　No herb, no living thing was there to see,
Only the rocks, the waters, and the sky.

The waves of years had smoothed a narrow ledge
 With age long beating on the earth's rough bound,
 And there I wandered from our camping ground,
And watched the ripple fretting at the edge.

Then I grew 'ware how by that twilight creek
 An old man sat and stared across the seas,
 Steadfast, with arms that rested on his knees,
And hollow hands that propped a hoary cheek;

His hair was white, his beard was grizzled grey,
 Yet was a fresh sea-keenness in his eyes
 That rose not, fell not, nor betrayed surprise,
But ever watched the fading track of day.

His garb was strange, and stained, and rent, and old,
 And I could see, for all the light was dim,
 That he was great and strong, and stout of limb,
And surely fashioned in heroic mould.

And rather to himself I thought than me,
 Softly and musingly he seemed to speak,
 In rhythmic measure of the yore-world Greek
That has the cadence of the lapping sea.

" Lo, I am he that could not drink his fill
　　　Of earthly knowledge in his little span,
　　　Who craved a lot too great for common man, —
　　I am Odysseus, and I wander still.

" The world, methinks, grows very old, the years
　　　Write deeper furrows in the sea-cliff's face ;
　　　Change ! change in all, save in the human race,
　　The same old passions and old loves and tears.

" They come and go—the little dust and breath—
　　　Whose only knowledge is that all things pass,
　　　And with that little dust at times, alas !
　　A spirit nobler than its doom of death.

" Man cannot pass outside the common lot,
　　　The worm that crawleth hath no use for wings ;
　　　I might have taught them many strange new things,
　　Old things forgotten, but they hearkened not.

" Earth has no use for me, I go no more
　　　Into the valleys and the tracks of men ;
　　　And now the seas are crowded out of ken,
　　And alien faces throng along the shore.

" I think Athena is long dead, or sleeps,
    Grown callous, but the grim Poseidon still
    Lives on, and drives me at his wanton will
By barren shallows and by pathless deeps.

" For ever in some little lonely bay
    I pass the friendless daylight, till the dark
    Shows forth the beacons of the night that mark
My westward course towards the dying day ;

" Then on and on into the sunset track,
    To where I have the blessed hope to die,
    To where the islands of the heroes lie,
But he relentless ever beats me back.

" Thus once or twice I have descried from far,
    A faint grey shadow in the morning haze,
    The outlines of my native land, the bays,
The long sought hills, beneath a waning star.

" The land I won and knew not how to keep,
    Wearying of ease, the altar and the loom,
    The thralls, the banquet, weary to my doom,
For I am weary, weary of the deep.

" I am as old as the world's age, well nigh,
   Too old for effort and too tired for strife,
   For ever drifting round the fringe of life,
And worn with waiting for the day to die."

Thus while he spoke he rose to his full height,
   Making a blank between the stars and me,
   Waded a little space into the sea
And vanished in the shadow of the night.

But softly like the echo of a sigh
   Came back as though upon a wind asleep,
   " For I am weary, weary of the deep,
And worn with waiting for the day to die."

Then, in a little while across the bay,
   I heard a plash like spirit oars, that broke
   Upon the stillness with a measured stroke,
Fainter and fainter till it passed away.

IN MAINA, 1890.

THE DREAM OF PHIDIAS.

COME in and see these marble gods of mine,
Finished and fair now, fit to take their place!
The hand's achievement, if not all the heart's,
As first it flashed forth in the fever glow.
Not yet, Aspasia, has the fire of youth
Died out so wholly ; I still try to dream
The hand must answer to the heart some day,
Art compass my ideal.   Vain, I know,
The thought, but I must cling to it.   If aught
Of life and might and majesty illume
These marble shapes, bethink you how they moved
Divine and dreadful in the artist's soul !
Not yet !—though years increase, and age, they say,
Reveals to man the measure of his might,
Restrains youth's wild ambitions, so we may
Grow perfect in the attainable, nor waste
The pith of manhood pining for the star.
But while I may I'll wrestle with my dream !

Oh, there are times I madden at the thought
Of impotence to render what I know ;
Always this long laborious process, years
And pains that go to do one small thing well,
The poor and partial triumph at the best ;
And all the while new visions lure in vain.
So hears the poet in his soul the sounds
Mystic, divine, and awful; on his lips
Only confused low murmuring of high things,
Not one untroubled echo of delight.
I can conceive a life let go in dreams
From sheer despair of saving what it sees.
Why are we made so—to behold at times
The heavens open, feel the giant's soul
All capable, with man's weak wearying hand
To grope and struggle in its orb confined
After the shape that glorified the dream ?

Well, dreams are dreams.   I had a dream one day;
I had gone up into the marble hill
To watch the quarrying, mark what blocks might be
Fair grained and flawless for this work of mine,
And it was sultry on the heights, and noon,

When great Pan sleeps aweary from the chase,
Men say, and pause is on the summer world.
There is a little deep-cut rock ravine,
Cooled with fresh water of perennial springs,
Hidden and low under the burning slopes,
Where summer through the oleanders blow
Rose-red among the shadows, and the air
Is lightly scented with the myrtle bloom ;
And thither wandering as chance would, alone,
I made the thyme my pillow, and with face
Turned to Pentelikon, I fell asleep,
And sleeping dreamed.

          There in my dream I saw
The mighty gable of the mountain brow
Gleam all one marble surface, smoothed and fair,
Huge and refulgent in the summer sun,
Shaped like the pediment of some vast shrine
For heroes' worship ; and I saw and felt,
Like a great sweep of music through my soul,
The artist's inspiration.   Grandly grouped
Ranged the immortals in an awful line,
A revelation on an arc of sky.

There in the midst arose the unconceived,

The vast and ancient Ouranos, o'erbowed

To snatch the laughing Earth into his breast,

Earth, the new mother, reaching forth her arms

And straining upward her surrendered lips,

Led on by Love, the oldest of all gods,

And evermore the youngest, Love, the life

Of all things living, wedding earth to sky.

And in the wake of Ouranos, the Winds,

An eager rout of lustiness and life,

The Season's sequence, and the dance of Hours,

The maiden keepers of the gate of heaven

Kissing the rosy fingers of the Dawn—

All these sprang into being; and beyond

Upreared the fiery coursers of the sun,

Spurning the æther with immortal feet,

Mounting and mounting.   So in Earth's fair train

Followed her sons the mountains, and the brood

Earth-born that haunt the forests and the rills,

And all the streams that issue from her breast—

A living ripple from the rock's white heart —

And all the rivers of the world drew on

To Ocean rising on a marble wave

Throned on the car that shakes the rooted hills
And girdles round creation.   After these
Was hoary Kronos, with the shadowy eyes
Bent down with weight of ages ; kneeling o'er
The form of Rhea, and for counterpart
Night sank at rest into the veiled embrace
Of Erebos, on the other side of day, —
The night of time behind the life and light,
Bounding the term of knowledge, for beyond
Where Tartaros, the dim unfathomed void,
Should be, lay Death, and on the other side
His brother Sleep, with wings about his brow,
And drooping eyes that watch across a dream.
All these I saw, each in his proper place,
Huge and immortal, as a god should stand ;
And every metope showed a glorious form—
Man, in the morning of his youth and strength,
Under the gods, but not a whit less fair ;
For all this meant the truce of God with man,
The miracle of life, the glory of the world.

Then a voice cried to me, " Arise, conform
The hand's achievement to the heart's desire ! "

And I was lifted with a giant's strength,
A giant's arm against the gleaming wall
Moving about it on the wings of air ;
And the white marble rained to earth like snow
Freed by the spring winds as I hacked and hewed
Shaping the thoughts that billowed through my brain.
Time I knew not, nor effort, but the hand
Answered the spirit as a ship the helm,
Till all the mountain grew instinct with life
As at my bidding. When I paused at last
The sun lay on the crags of Salamis,
And I surveyed my finished work, the glow
Gilding the marble forehead of the gods,
The realized conception. One great throb
Of gladness went up through the artist's soul,
And once on earth dreaming I was content.
Then lo, I saw how it was lifted up
On blue pilasters of the evening sky,
In the sun's face, crowned with the dawning stars,
Dwarfing mankind's achievement, vast, sublime
Worthy of God, and worthy that ideal
God spurs man ever vainly to pursue.

When I awoke it was all twilight round ;
The misted purple of the mountain-peak
Looked far ethereal, pointing to a star,
As though it yearned to reach it, and in vain ;
But near it broadened to the breast of earth
With long strong arms that gathered in the plain.
The silent pathos touched me, and I found
A solace for my vanished dream ; for while
The summit strained toward the unreached star,
Deep in the earth its strong foundations lay.
And so, Aspasia, will I keep my dreams
And still aspire, if vainly ! but no less
Perfect this hand within its lowlier sphere,
Be strong in my own strength, and compass here
Some part maybe of things attainable
Before the twilight closes to the night.

PENTELIKON, 1889.

TANAGRA.

WE rode through mellowing cornlands, deep ravines,
  By torrent beds where oleanders nod,
Up paths of arbutus and evergreens,
  And flowery carpets that no feet have trod.

Yet all this lonely land is holy ground,
  Strewn with dead dust of cities, such an one
You chance upon, a low wall ringing round
  The wilderness of thistle, grass and stone.

There rose the citadel, these mounds were streets,
  That crescent hill was where the actors played,
The lentisk bushes have usurped the seats
  Where camps the Wallack goatherd in the shade.

And this was Tanagra, this waste of weed,
  These hillocks with the buried life within,
A few rough gravestones keep their names to read—
  One broken fragment bore the name Corinne.

Ah ! scarcely hers whose flawless face and fame
   The old world wondered at, a lordlier grave
Enshrined in death those lyric lips, whose name
   Is all of her that after years might save.

Yet here, where once she saw the living light
   And struck the chord of passion, there it lay,
And that mere word upon the stone had might,
   A moment's space to flash the dark to-day.

To dreams of fanes bedecked with myrtle boughs,
   Dreams of the Theban contest and the prize,
The laurel snatched from Pindar's throbbing brows,
   And bound above a minstrel maiden's eyes.

Was it the music wholly or the grace
   For which the swan of Dirce drooped his wing,
The fount of passion, or the fair, fair face,
   While Thebes was mute to hear a woman sing ?

Ringed sit the priests, the judges of the song,
   The maiden muse stands passion-pale between,
Loud for the Theban, louder and more long,
   Break forth the plaudits for the Tanagrine.

There winds the glad procession, the white row
　　Of virgin escort up the marble street,
The twin-pipes pealing shrilly as they go,
　　To lay the tripod at the song-god's feet !

Such power the dead voice had ! **long years** have kept
　　No note of songs that filled the mouth of fame,
No record how she loved or laughed or wept,
　　Naught but the face, the triumph, and the name.

These and what dreams memorial lands still keep,
　　Where mighty presences have passed and been,
Where Leucas shows the Lesbian's lover-leap,
　　Where Tanagra still whispers of Corinne.

TANAGRA, 1889.

THE SONG OF THE KLEPHT.

The red fire flickered through the sea-bound cave,
A lamb was roasting on the spit—the wave
Broke low and soothing round the sandy bay,
And on the sky-line hung the ghost of day.
Ringèd round the fire we sat, the wine-cup passed
From each to other—no one spoke at last.

Old Janni in the linen kilt, with red
Rough-knotted kerchief round his grizzled head,
And mighty cloak of goat's frieze, mused and rolled
The paper round Agrinion's weed of gold,
Then snatched an ember from the thyme-root fire,
And blew the smoke in cloudy wreaths.

                                          His Sire

Was with Odysseus on the mountain side
In the wild days before the land was free ;
Such war-songs rocked his cradle, when the bride
Would sling beneath the dark vallonea tree
Her infant's leather hammock :—

                                        So sang he.

What has become of Dimos, the Dimos that we
    knew,

Who never missed the mark he aimed, whose blade
    was keen and true,

Who wore the silver pistols, the shoulder-bits of gold,

The golden braided jacket, and the kilt of treble
    fold.

He left our high liméri, he drew the lot and went

To tell the rest in Agrapha our powder stores were
    spent.

He was not gone an hour, an hour by the sun,

When a distant shot rang up the hills, and then another
    one ;

We sprang to foot and listened, held breath and
    dropped the lyre,

We heard a hundred echoes take up the running fire ;

And through the thymy boulders in cover of the
    trees,

We slid along the broken ledge, and crawled upon
    our knees,

Until we saw the vultures come sailing up the blue,

And circle round the rocky gorge, his way went
    winding through.

And there lay two Liápids, a hundred feet apart,

The first was stark and not quite cold, with a bullet
   through his heart ;

And one had fallen headlong, from out the torrent
   bed

His rigid eyes stared grimly, and he was not quite
   dead;

The silent curse was on his lips, and round his
   matted hair

A purple stain ran down the stones—but Dimos was
   not there.

The earth was dry, the rocks were bare, and track
   was none to find,

Did they bear the living with them, and leave their
   dead behind ?

His mother from the village comes like a thing bereft,

And wanders round the hollow hills through the
   eyries of the Klepht,

And "have you seen my Dimos, have you seen my
   bonny son,

Who wore the Aga's pistols and the silver-mounted
   gun ?

My curse on you black mountain, dark gorge and
    river bed,

You took my Dimos living, and you hide him from
    me dead !"

There's an eagle 'lit on Pindus with dripping beak
    and red,

Between his crimson talons, he holds a severed head,

He feasts upon the olive eyes that lack their lustre-
    light,

And keener grows a hundredfold the orbit of his
    sight.

He cracks the skull in pieces and picks the scattered
    brain,

And fiercer grows his courage and more his might
    and main,

He feels his pinions stronger and longer many spans,

With the strength and youth and hardihood that
    were the murdered man's.

Oh, Ali, dog of Jannina, the headsman of the east,

Chimári well remembers who makes the eagles' feast !

ZALONGOS.

THE LAST FIGHT OF SULI.

ZALONGOS was the mountain height
Where Suli's star went down in night,
The star that kindled as it fell
A flame on freedom's citadel ;
Which flashed across from sea to sea
The signal-fire of liberty.

Through twenty years of battle
    They kept the dog at bay,
The dog that rules in Jannina,
    And sends his sons to slay :
And never Suliote maiden,
    And never captive wife,
Had sold to false Liápids
    Her honour for her life ;
But the pharas of the mountain
    Were ever thin and few,

And traitors grow in every soil
　　When gold can find the clue.

He had promised peace to Suli,
　　The terms were meet and fair,
And when they trusted in his bond
　　Fell on them unaware.
There are none in Avaríkos,
　　In Kako-Suli none,
Kiunghi's rafters smoulder yet,
　　Kiápha has not one.
In Jannina in the market place
　　Their heads are stacked in piles,
And Ali the dog in his palace
　　Counts over them and smiles.
But the last and best of Suli
　　Will never yield nor fly,
And these will keep Zalongos' steep,
　　Or show the way to die.

And deadly was the fusillade
Those roving mountain marksmen made ;
From clump to clump of lentisk green,
Through splintered rocks they glide unseen ;

And flint and steel struck never spark
To speed the ball that missed its mark,
Yet on and on the Pasha's ranks
Drew slowly up the mountain flanks.

The rugged peaks are wild and sheer
As Suli's eagle eyries here,
With dark defiles of narrow span,
And boulder rocks that mask a man.
But what should those few hundreds do !
For not one thousand came, nor two,
But five, and ten, and thousands more
Press on where these have gone before,
Till every mountain path and spur,
And every slope of stunted fir,
And every gorge and every glen
Is swarming with the kilted men.

From morn to noon the battle grew,
Till midday blazed from out the blue,
While hidden hands that never tire
Pour down the slope a dropping fire ;
And aye, as Suli's sons retreat
They burn the scrub beneath their feet,

Till higher, higher, bare and black,
A ring that narrowed marked their track ;
Yet on and on, through smoke and flame,
The hounds of Vizir Ali came.

Then noon went by, and up the ridge
   The sun struck ruby red,
But redder on Zalongos' side
   Was the blood of Ali's dead ;
Then the dark shadows deepened,
   And the pale stars grew bright,
A mist rose up the gorges,
   And sudden fell the night ;
But still those echoes rang with cries,
Of dying men in agonies,
Wild shrieks to those who answer not,
And rattle of the musket shot.

The night went by—each volley's crash,
Revealed new foemen by the flash,
And every time the flash struck red
Some mountain bullet claimed its dead ;
Yet evermore the burning slope
Shut out another door of hope,

For close behind the moving flame
Fresh hordes of those Liápids came,
Till through the bloody mist and smoke
The second dawn of battle broke.

Upon a high rock platform
  Hard by the summit's crest,
The Suliote mothers sat and watched
  Their babies at the breast ;
The mountain rim dropped sheer and grim
  From that high citadel
To where far down in murk and gloom
Deep furrowed runs the stream of doom
  That has its source in hell.
They waited for the morning sun —
They saw the heights were lost and won,
And Suli's star, long clouded o'er,
Had set in blood for evermore ;
And vain it were to suckle braves,
And end as demon Ali's slaves !

What words were said, what grim debate,
  No man will ever know ;

The firing still rang up the rocks,
  And muttered back below.
They did not weep, nor tear the hair,
Betray one gesture of despair,
  But with a seeming mute accord
    They rose up in a row.
Men saw each mother snatch her child
    To one long clinging kiss,
A kiss to keep, a kiss to sleep,
Then fling them down the horrid deep
    Of Acheron's abyss.
Their lives the mountains cradled,
    Freedom the mountains gave,
So in the mountains' hollow arms
    Be the free Suliote's grave !

Their foes shall see with bated breath
How Suli's women welcome death
    Unshrived of living priest,
While round their feet the muskets peal,
And overhead the vultures wheel,
    Impatient for the feast.

Then linking hands one last time more
They trod the Syrtos dance of yore—
The dance that oft on eves of spring
Would draw them round its magic ring
By Kako-Suli's frowning doors
Or Avaríko's threshing-floors,
While weirdly chanted shrill and strong,
Defiant rose the dancing-song.

But ever as the ring wound round
Towards the bastion's outer bound,
The waving chain a moment stands,
The last unlinks her clinging hands,
And moving on in rhythmic grace
Leaps over into space.
Nor ever one looked down the edge
Of that sheer eagle-haunted ledge
To mark what trace along the steep
Of those who took the horrid leap,
But dancing to the dancing strain,
Shrill o'er the bullets' iron rain,
The last one still with tearless face
Shoots out in order from her place,

Till only ten, till five, and four
Are left to tread the measure o'er.
The foes draw near; oh, haste! make haste!
Till three, and two, and one at last,
Who, like some Mænad god-possessed,
Shrieks the wild death-song o'er the rest,
The dirge of Suli, and her own,
Then plunges headlong down, alone.

And what of those who still were left
To hold the eyrie of the Klepht?
A few with Bòtzaris to guide
Shall breast and break the deathly tide,
And win to where the road is free,
Toward Parga and the island sea;
A few shall cleave a bloody path
Across the closing ring,
To venge as freedom's aftermath,
This carnage of the spring;
To sit perhaps at Byron's door,
And tell this story o'er and o'er,
To still defy the hornèd moon,
By Misolonghi's wan lagoon,

And yet may be in direr need
To man the breach and fight and bleed,
And dare another hero-deed.

But thus beneath Zalongos' side
The mothers and the children died,
That Suli ne'er might breed again
A race of less heroic men.

1891.

THE LUTE OF ORPHEUS.

ORPHEUS dead, the Thracian Mænads left him lying
    marble-pale,
Thrust the daggers through their hair-knots, shrieking,
    fled along the vale.

But the still face in the rushes and the eyes that had
    no sight
Stared with pitiful appealing through the shadows of
    the night.

And the night-bird missed his answer, and a sadness
    marred her song,
And the wind sighed in the willows, and the stream
    bewailed his wrong.

And the clouds swept tears for sorrow, and the wan
    moon veiled her eyes,
For the sob of stricken nature seemed to penetrate the
    skies.

There one found him who had loved him, in the reed-
    bed gashed and torn,
Where of old she heard him singing in the silence of
    the morn ;

Found her hero far-off worshipped, dimly known and
    deified,
Found the magic lute beside him and the lute-strings
    all untied.

Bent a laurel bough to crown him, smoothed the
    damp hair on his head,
Closed the startled eyes, and gently kissed the cold
    lips of her dead.

And she decked the corse with rushes, hid the red and
    horrid scars,
Said, "Oh, silent voice of music, re-awakened with the
    stars,

When up there at Zeus' high feasting, crowned you
    strike a louder lute,
Seeing all things, oh remember one whose love was
    meek and mute.

Then the Muses came lamenting by the Strymon's
    willowy shore,
Wept immortal tears bewailing, " Worship is on earth
    no more.

" Thou that lovedst, thou that weepest, thine unsatis-
    fied desire
Shall rewake the broken music of the silent singer's
    lyre.

" Sing of love as he of beauty, sing of tears as he of
    mirth,
Sing of peace as he of passion, sing the woman-song
    of earth."

So they twined their hair for lute-strings, kissed unrest
    into her eyes,
Bared her soul to human sorrow, tuned her lips to
    human sighs.

And they sped her forth to wander, touching mortal
    hearts to tears,
First on earth of maiden singers in the morning of the
    years.

CALLISTE.

In May, when oleanders bloom,
What time the gold was on the broom,
Before the moon was full above,
A world that seemed but made for love,
When glow-worms lit the way we went
To bruise the hill thyme into scent,
The shadows of your raven hair,
The charm of movements free as air,
Your wild bird grace of shy replies,
The mischief in your sea-deep eyes,
Had tempted me to whisper you
The word world-old, but ever new,
The word that seemed so light to say
When oleanders bloomed in May.

But, ah, Calliste, over sea
The fickle wind sets where for me
Lie other ways and other cares ;—

F

For you the soft Ægean airs,
The sails in yonder haven furled
To tell you of the outside world,
The starry nights, the spring's perfume
Returning with the orange bloom,
The simple prayer you know to pray,
The ready mirth, and then some day
Some sailor with the broad brown chest
To snatch the flower from your breast,
To knot his fingers in your hair,
Draw up your face and call it fair,
And say the word I dared not say
When oleanders bloomed in May.

FOLK SONGS.

(*From the Romaic.*)

Why are the mountains dark and the hills all
woebegone ?

Is it the wind at war there or the rain that blots the
sun ?

It is not the wind at war there, it is not the driving
rain,

It is Charos passing over them, with the dead folk in
his train ;

The old men follow after, and before the young men
go,

And the children, the little children, are slung at his
saddle bow ;—

The old men beg a grace of him, and the young men
speak him fair ;

"Good Charos rest by the fountain, or halt in the
village square,

That the lads may play at the stone throwing, and the
   old men drink their fill,

That the children may go and gather the wild flowers
   on the hill."

The old men beg a grace of him, and the young men
   speak him fair :—

" By never a fountain will I rest, nor halt in the
   village square ;

The mothers would come for water, and would hear
   their babes complain,

And the wedded folk would never part, if they once
   were met again."

———

God made so many good things, but one thing made
   not well ;

He made no bridge to cross the sea, no ladder down
   to hell ;

That one might cross and find a way to get to the
   dead folk there,

And see how the little children that have got no
   mothers fare.

———

On the stream of life, oh say,
Wherefore did you come my way?
Since to meet was but to sever,
Wherefore did I meet you ever?
Since you only taught me after
   That a lover's sighs are deep,
Since my tears but move your laughter,
   Though it be for you I weep.
Give me life, or pass my sentence,
   Let it cease this weary breath!
Haply then in late repentance,
   You will soften touched by death.
Little grace I crave—my pain
Will not turn your heart again—
Only this, where fleeting fast,
These my days are told at last,
Breathe one farewell in a sigh,
Let one tear fall where I lie.

CHRISTMAS IN THE ÆGEAN.

It is the eve of Christmas in the world,
　　But gentle as a morn of spring,—the deep
　　One opal to the sky-line, as in sleep
Drifts past the seagull with her wide wings furled.

We floated on between the isles that lie
　　Like leaves of lilies in a summer mere,
　　And dreamed no storm wind ever ventured near
This zone of peace between the sea and sky.

We dreamed of golden galleys and of quays
　　Bright with their burden of long colonnades,
　　The shrines of Passion and the mystic glades,
The siren cities of the Cyclades.

Where are the island voices now? The mirth
　　Is dead or silent ; no mad laughter thrills
　　The dance of Oreads in the happy hills
Where twilight settles on a sadder earth.

For here on that first Christmas eve, men said
　　They heard a sound like sobbing in the breeze,
　　A sound that scared the fisher from the seas,
A wail blown earthward, crying, " Pan is dead ! "

The feet of time have touched the rocky shore,
　　There is a change behind the changelessness,
　　The suns of summer warm the world no less,
But the light heart of morning,—never more !

So day went down behind the ocean rim,
　　While westward the sweet star of silence grew
　　Through yellow hazes melting into blue ;
The shadows deepened till the isles were dim.

Then like a soul forsaken, hushed in fright
　　The dark world seemed to pause, no ripple broke,
　　No wind, no voice of earth or ocean spoke,
While the stars watched from the great arch of night ;

Till faintly eastward flushed the hope of morn,
　　Pale with one star prevailing, till the grey
　　Lifted, the new sun triumphed, and strong day
Woke with a song voice, crying, " Christ is born ! "

　　1889.

AKROTIRI OF CRETE.

THERE is a rocky half isle in the deep
With jagged peaks, with sea-walls bare and steep ;
With scanty pasture for the goats that climb
From ledge to ledge, and bruise the mountain thyme,
Only dwarf holly and low lentisk clings
In hollows sheltered from the north wind's wings,
Dark gullies where the mountain vultures sway
On poising pinions, watching for their prey,
For hunted beasts will find their way to die
In such a solitude 'twixt earth and sky.
A stony desert parts that land unkind
From green Cydonia's summer world behind,
Where ancient olives silver the rich plain,
Ringed in their fence of aloes, till again
The vine-slopes climb to Ida's mountain chain.

And yet there is a green spot in this waste,
A garden in the desert, man has placed

An altar in the solitude, come here to dwell
With contemplation in a hermit's cell.
Long years ago men counted this their good,
Fled from the world's way, chose the solitude,
Went out into the deserts, barefoot trod
The rocks that bruised them, agonized to God,
Welcomed the lash, the torture and the chain,
And dreamed of heaven in the pause of pain.
But now, dear God, has love not cast out fear?
These lonely eremites, what do they here?

Enter thou in between the cypress rows,
Mount up the stair ;—four terraced walls enclose
A court, the church, a citron by the well ;—
Is it a fortress or a cloister cell?
Speak with those hermits,—have they thoughts to think
Worthy this deep seclusion?   Do they drink
A deeper well of knowledge?   Bearded cheek,
Locks like the Nazzarite, do they bespeak
Mystics, who commune oft with God below,
The priests of contemplation?   Surely,—No!
Ask, you will find them ignorant and poor
A few rude peasants in a cowl, no more!

What do they here, walled sullenly within,
Secure at ease while others toil and spin ?
What do they here, men stout and strong of limb,
Between the matin and the vesper hymn ?
Fasting or feasting, letting real life go,
While other men must dig and reap and sow,
Smiling their welcome to who comes their way
With half-remembered empty forms to pray !
Is this man's portion, between earth and sky,
To crawl in indolence, to live and die ?

And yet not so ! Be patient, being wise,
Nay, proud, not patient ; learn to recognize
The dawnings of endeavour, the good seed
Sown in a land that knows its hunger's need.
Here, where the passions of her sons are rude,
And fierce as nature's in her wildest mood,
Where hate is painted with the blood she spills,
And murder harbours in the savage hills,
It was well thought to build this home of peace,
To watch the olives and the vines increase,
Where, unmolested in a world of strife,
Unlettered hermits lead the quiet life.

So slowly men mount upwards.   Be their praise

This garden island in the stony ways,

Where flocks feed quietly, birds build and sing,

Men sleep unscared beneath the shadow of God's
wing.

CRETE, 1889.

THE CYCLADES.

THE summer seas lie smooth and fair,
The pause of sunrise holds the air,
The canvas woos the wind in vain
That chased the moon and dropped again ;
All round us on the pearly deep
Dim forms of islands seem to sleep,
For suns of morning hardly break
Their truce of silence when they wake,
Whom years of woes have taught to bless
The peace of sweet forgetfulness.

Oh summer isles, whose young desires
Were music once on living lyres,
What time the Teian made divine
His wreath of roses drenched in wine,
The Lesbian sang her woman's woe
In bars of passion we but know,
Across a void of silence drear

From other hearts that throbbed to hear,
What ills untold make up the sum
That struck your soul of music dumb,
Through all the ages dark with crime
When earth was in her travail time !—
Her virgin youth was sunned with smiles
In these blue wave-engirdled isles,
But passion came, and youth went by,
The golden age was quick to die.

From west and east what white sails came
Whose only freight was sword and flame,
Beflagged with Crescent or with Cross,
Whose either gain was human loss !
Oh fierce red years of ruth and wrong,
You ill befit a summer song !
The smoking homes, the parting cries,
The hell let loose on paradise,
The lonely lives in alien lands,
The wrenched embrace of clinging hands,
When men were slain and women slaved,
Who death in better boon had craved,
While dread o'ershadowed every morn,

And night fell on a world forlorn,
The naked to the mountains fled,
And all the wells were choked with dead !

Ah me, the fair things made for joy
It needed ages to destroy,
The colonnades on marble quays,
The valleys cool with waving trees,
The terraced orchards up the hill,
The shrines we might have worshipped still,
The statues in the myrtle glade !
But man has marred what man had made,
What God and man had best combined,
And left the barren rocks behind.

The waves have washed the blood away
And ocean smiles her best to-day,
But will the voices wake once more
That made such music heretofore ?
It echoes still across the tears
Of twice a thousand silent years.
Ah, surely, world of summer isles,
For hearts are here and woman's smiles,

And dreams to dream, and deeds to do,
And years of ruin to renew ;
The last wild storm has passed to peace,
It found you still the soul of Greece.

Off Nios, 1890.

PENTELIKON.

TO C. M. M.

I THINK the memory I love best
   Is one of Attic stars
On old Pentele's marble breast
   Among her quarried scars;
When fierce day died a cooler breeze
Would steal across our poplar trees,
   And westward bring the breath of seas.

And when the moons grew full and fair
   They drew us forth to climb
The path that seemed a marble stair
   Between the tufted thyme ;
Those stars hung down so large and nigh,
Far closer to the earth than sky,
   And we were silent, you and I.

We scaled the rugged crest and lay
   On nature's thymy bed,

To watch the meteors at their play
  In sapphire deeps o'erhead,
To dream strange forms moved to and fro
The crescent plain that lay below,
  The ghosts of battle long ago.

There earth and sea lay side by side
  Beneath in summer sleep,
And shadowy islands dim descried
  Showed o'er a shadowy deep:
And waves of mountain faintly white
Rose up from mist-worlds out of sight,
  Like crowns of crystal in the night.

Then slowly east to watching eyes
  A band of rainbow red
Grew o'er the bound of seas and skies,
  And the stars paled and fled,
While through the flush, light aureoled,
Up sailed a sphere of molten gold,
  And down the bay the glory rolled.

Isle after island rose to ken
  Beneath that ruby band

G

And amber waves came racing in
   To tell the sleeping land,
The scattered mists wreathed up in smoke,
Through purple gorges morning broke,
   And all the rugged mountain woke.

The hound that night through vigil kept
   Gave one deep warning note,
The shepherd rose from where he slept,
   And shook his white capote ;
Far down beneath the watch dogs bay,
The goats spring up the pasture way,
   And in a moment all is day.

Ah, those were nights, those Attic nights,
   On old Pentele's brow !
Long days to me of keen delights,
   Those summer days !—By now,
The myrtle sheds its bloom like snows,
The oleander buds unclose
   New clusters of the ruddy rose ;

The fountain from the marble's breast
   Leaps forth as fresh and fair,

The wind at eve still wanders west,

    Though we be no more there ;

For us the suns of Greece have set,

But I at least remember yet,

    And tune my music to regret.

ROME, 1891.

HELLAS.

It is not only that the sun
    Loves best these southern lands,
It is not for the trophies won
    Of old by hero hands,
That nature wreathed in softer smiles
    Was here the bride of art;
A closer kinship claims these isles,
    The love-land of the heart.
It is because the poet's dream
    Still haunts each happy vale,
That peopled every grove and stream
    To fit his fairy tale.

There may be greener vales and hills
    Less bare to shelter man;
But still they want the naiad rills,
    And miss the pipe of Pan.
There may be other isles as fair

And summer seas as blue,
But then Odysseus touched not there,
   Nor Argo beached her crew.
For me the Nereid-haunted shore,
   The Faun-frequented dell,
Can wake the note of wonder more
   Than stones where Cæsars fell:
And where the blooms of Zante blow
   Their incense to the waves;
Where Ithaca's dark headlands show
   The legendary caves;
Where in the deep of olive groves
   The summer hardly dies;
Where fair Phæacia's sun-brown maids
   Still keep their siren eyes;
Where Chalcis strains with loving lips
   Towards the little bay,
The strand that held the thousand ships,
   The Aulis of delay;
Where Œta's ridge of granite bars,
   The gate Thermopylæ,
Where huge Orion crowned with stars
   Looks down on Rhodope;

Where once Apollo tended flocks
   On Phera's lofty plain,
Where Peneus cleaves the stubborn rocks
   To find the outer main ;
Where Argos and Mycenæ sleep
   With all the buried wrong,
And where Arcadian uplands keep
   The antique shepherd song,
There is a spirit haunts the place
   All other lands must lack,
A speaking voice, a living grace,
   That beckons fancy back.

Dear isles and sea-indented shore,
   Till songs be no more sung,
The souls of singers gone before
   Shall keep your lovers young :
And men will hymn your haunted skies,
   And seek your holy streams,
Until the soul of music dies,
   And earth has done with dreams.

SONGS OF ENGLAND

(First Series).

———

TO MY FRIEND,

GEORGE CURZON.

" *Since you believe in that great work her sons have still to do,*
Persuaded that her service means the world's best service too,
These first-fruits of my English songs I dedicate to you."

SONGS OF ENGLAND.

SPRING THOUGHTS.

My England, island England, such leagues and leagues
    away,
It's years since I was with thee, when April wanes to
    May :—

Years since I saw the primrose, and watched the
    brown hillside
Put on white crowns of blossom and blush like April's
    bride ;

Years since I heard thy skylark, and caught the
    throbbing note
Which all the soul of springtide sends through the
    blackbird's throat.

Oh England, island England, if it has been my lot
To live long years in alien lands, with men who love
　　thee not,

I do but love thee better who know each wind that
　　blows,
The wind that slays the blossom, the wind that buds
　　the rose,

The wind that shakes the taper mast and keeps the
　　topsail furled,
The wind that braces nerve and arm to battle with the
　　world:

I love thy moss-deep grasses, thy great untortured
　　trees,
The cliffs that wall thy havens, the weed-scents of thy
　　seas,

The dreamy river reaches, the quiet English homes,
The milky path of sorel down which the springtide
　　comes.

Oh land so loved through length of years, so tended
    and caressed,
The land that never stranger wronged nor foeman
    dared to waste,

Remember those thou speedest forth round all the
    world to be
Thy witness to the nations, thy warders on the sea !

And keep for those who leave thee and find no better
    place
The olden smile of welcome, the unchanged mother-
    face !

Athens, 1890.

A BALLAD OF THE ARMADA.

1588—1888.

THERE shall be so much forgotten of deeds beneath
the sun,

But not this deed of England's, till England's race be
run ;

The fathers shall tell their children, and the children's
children know

How we fought the great sea-battle three hundred
years ago.

It was in the middle summer, and the wheat was full
in ear,

But men's hearts were dark and troubled, and
women's faint for fear :

The fleets of Spain set sail in May, but a storm had
warned them home,

The might of Spain had met again to do the will of
Rome.

The Pope's high benediction had sped them on their
way,

With monks and priests and bishops to teach us how
pray ;

And all the Southland's knighthood, well proved in
many a field,

And all her great sea-captains had come to make us
yield ;

And thirty thousand seamen and soldiers lay
aboard ;—

So England watched and waited, and trusted in the
Lord.

Then all along this southern coast there was
hurrying to and fro,

And the nation's eyes went seaward to watch the
coming foe ;

The shepherds left the pasture-hills, the yeomen left
their farms,

For all the squires in England were gathering men-at-
arms;

And there was vigil through the night, and ever stir
and life,

From the Foreland to the Landsend, before the
    coming strife ;

The old sea-dogs of England were met on Plymouth
    Hoe,

And the little fleet was anchored across the Sound
    below ;

And rusty swords were furbished while yet the corn
    was green,

For a mighty cry went through the land, *For God and
    for the Queen !*

It was a July evening, and in the waning day

The fairy woods of Edgcumbe hung rosy o'er the
    bay,

When through the track of sun-set, full-sail and home-
    ward bound,

A little bark came gliding in and anchored up the
    Sound ;

And round the quays and through the streets a wild-
    fire rumour ran,

A sea-league off the Lizard they've seen the Spanish
    van.

They say the Lord High Admiral was bowling on the
green,

And round him sat the goodliest men the world has
ever seen ;

For there was Richard Grenville, the bravest of the
brave,

Who fought the greatest sea-fight that ever shook the
wave ;

And there sat old John Hawkins, and preached of loot
and prize,

And the grim battle-hunger flashed through his
grizzled eyes ;

And there was Martin Frobisher, who tried the
North-west way,

And saw the sunless noontide, and saw the midnight
day ;

And Drake, the seaman's hero, whose sails were
never furled,

Whose bark had found the ocean-path that girdles
round the world ;

And Preston of La Guayra, and Fenner of the Azores,

Who shook the flag of England out on undiscovered
shores ;

And Fenton, and John Davis, and many another one,
Whose keels had ploughed the Spanish Main behind
the setting sun.
Without one dark misgiving they sat and watched the
play,
And sipped their wine and laughed their jests like
boys on a holiday.
That night men fired the beacons and flared the
message forth,
From the southland to the midland, from the midland
to the north :
And there was mustering all night long, wild rumour
and unrest,
And mothers clasped their children the closer to their
breast ;
But calmly yet in Plymouth Sound the fleet of
England lay,
The gunners slept beside their guns and waited for
the day.

Then as the mists of morning cleared, up drew the
Spanish van,
And grimly off the Devon cliffs that ten days' fight
began.

Four giant galleons led the way like vultures to the
feast,

And the huge league-long crescent rolled on from
west to east :

But they will not stay for Plymouth, nor check the
late advance,

For Parma's armies wait and fret to cross the Strait
from France.

No grander fleet, no better foe, has ever crossed the
main,

No braver captains walked the deck than hold the
day for Spain.

There sailed Miguel d'Oquenda, our seamen knew
him well,

Recalde and Pietro Valdez, Mexia and Pimentel.

Oh, if ever, men of England, now brace your courage
high,

Make good your boast to rule the waves, and keep the
linstocks dry :

For the weeks of weary waiting, the long alert is
past,

The pent-up hate of nations meets face to face at
last.

H

The giant ships held on their course, and as the last
was clear

The Plymouth fleet put out to sea and hung upon
their rear ;

And their war-drums beat to quarters, the bugles
blared alarms,

The stately ocean-castles were filled with men-at-arms.

All through that summer morn and noon, on till the
close of night,

We harried through the galleons and fought a
running fight ;

And far up Dartmoor highlands men heard the
booming gun,

And watched the clouds of battle beneath the summer
sun.

As o'er some dead sea-monster wheel round the white-
winged gulls,

Our little ships ran in and out between the giant
hulls ;

For fleetly through their clumsy lines we steered our
nimble craft,

And thundered in our broadsides, and raked them
fore and aft,

And broke their spars, and rammed their oars, till the
    floating castles reeled,
While overhead their cannon flashed, their idle volleys
    pealed.
And the sun went down behind us, but the sea was ·
    ribbed with red,
For the greatest of the galleons was burning as she
    fled.
Yet hard behind we followed and held on through the
    night,
And kept the tossing lanterns of the Spanish fleet in
    sight.
So past Torbay to Portland Bill they ran on even
    keels,
And ever we hung behind them and gored their
    flying heels ;
And many a mastless galley was left alone to lag,
To fall back in the hornets' nest, and, fighting, strike
    her flag.
Then every port along the coast put out its
    privateers,
And one by one our ships came in with ringing
    cheers on cheers ;

So sailed Sir Walter Raleigh, the knight-errant of the
    sea,

And all the best of Cornwall and Devon's chivalry ;

Northumberland and Cumberland and Oxford and
    Carew,—

Till from every mast in England the red-cross banner
    blew.

A calm fell on the twenty fifth,—it was St. Jago's
    day,—

And face to face off Weymouth cliffs the baffled war-
    ships lay.

Now, bishops, read your masses, and, friars, chant
    your psalm !

Now, Spain, go up and prosper, for your saint hath
    sent the calm !

A thousand oars that move like one lash white the
    glassy blue,

And down their three great galleons bore towards our
    foremost few.

Then loud laughed Admiral Howard, and a cheer
    went up the skies,

King Philip's three great galleons will be a noble prize !

So we towed out two of our six ships to meet each
floating fort,

And we laid one on the starboard side and we laid one
on the port ;

And all forenoon we pounded them ; they fought us
hard and well,

Till the sulphur-clouds along the calm hung like the
breath of hell :

But a fair wind rose at noontide and baulked us of
our prey,

The rescue came on wings of need and snatched the
prize away ;

So past the Needles, past Spithead, along the Sussex
shores,

The tide of battle eastward rolls, the cannon's thunder
roars ;

The pike-men on the Sussex Downs could see the
running fight,

And spread the rumour inland, the Dons were full in
flight :

The fishing-smacks put out to sea from many a white
chalk cove

To follow in the battle's wake and glean the treasure-
　　trove ;
Till night fell on the battle-scene, and under moon
　　and star
Men saw the English Channel all one long flame of
　　war.

So, harried like their hunted bulls before the
　　horsemen's goad,
They dropped on the eve of Sunday to their place in
　　Calais road :
And we, we ringed about them and dogged them to
　　their lair
Beneath the guns of Calais, to fight us if they dare ;
But afar they rode at anchor and rued their battered
　　pride,
As a wounded hound draws off alone to lick his gory
　　side ;
And when the Sabbath morning broke, they had not
　　changed their line,
For Parma's host by Dunkirk town lay still and made
　　no sign.

So calm that Sabbath morning fell, men heard the
    land-bells ring,

They heard the monks at masses, the Spanish soldiers
    sing;

And as the moon grew sultry came other sounds of
    mirth,

And when the sun set many had seen the last on
    earth.

A breeze sprang up at even, and the clouds rolled up
    the sky,

And dark and boding fell the night, that last night of
    July.

But in the fleet of England was every soul awake,

For a pinnace ran from bark to bark and brought us
    word from Drake ;

And we towed eight ships to leeward, and set their
    bows to shore,

To send the dons a greeting they never had before ;

No traitor moon revealed us, there shone no summer
    star

As we smeared the doomed hulls over with rosin
    and with tar ;

And all their heavy ordnance was rammed with stone
and chain,

And they bore down on the night wind into the heart
of Spain.

It was Prowse and Young of Bideford who had the
charge to steer,

And a bow shot from the Spanish lines they fired
them with a cheer,

Dropped each into his pinnace—it was deftly done
and well—

And on the tide set shoreward they loosed the floating
hell !

Oh, then were cables severed, then rose a panic
cry

To every saint in heaven, that shook the reddened
sky !

And some to north and some to south, like a herd of
bulls set free,

With sails half set and cracking spars they staggered
out to sea :

But we lay still in order and ringed them as they came,

And scared the cloudy dawning with thunder and with
flame.

The North Sea fleet came sailing down, our ships grew
more and more,

As Winter charged their severed van and drove their
best on shore.

The Flemish boors came out to loot, and up the
Holland dykes

The windmills stopped, the burghers marched with
muskets and with pikes ;

So we chased them through the racing sea and banged
them as they went,

And some we sank, and boarded some, till all our shot
was spent ;

Till we had no food nor powder, but only the will to
fight,

And the shadows closed about us and we lost them in
the night.

The white sea-horses sniffed the gale and climbed our
sides for glee,

And rocked us and caressed us and danced away to lee.

Now rest you, men of England, for the fight is lost
and won,

The God of Storms will do the rest, and grimly it was
done ;

Far north, far north on wings of death those
    scattered galleys steer

Towards the rock-bound islands, the Scottish headlands
    drear ;

And the fishers of the Orkneys shall reap a golden
    store,

And Irish kernes shall strip the dead tossed up their
    rocky shore.

Long, long the maids of Aragon may watch and wait
    in vain,

The boys they sent for dowries will never come again.

Deep, fathom deep their lovers sleep beneath an alien
    wave,

And not a foot of English land, not even for a grave !

But it's Ah for the childless mothers ! and Ah for the
    widowed maids !

And the sea-weed, not the myrtle, twined round their
    rusting blades !

    But we sailed back in triumph, our banner floating
        free,

Our lion-banner in the gale,—the masters of the sea !

The waves did battle for us, the winds were on our
   side,

The God of the just and unjust hath humbled Philip's
   pride.

Henceforth shall no man bind us: where'er the salt
   tides flow

Our sails shall take the sea-breeze, the oaks of England
   go !

And every isle shall know them, and every land that
   lies

Beyond the bars of sunset, the shadows of sunrise.

Henceforth, oh Island England, be worthy of thy fate,

And let thy new-world children revere thee wise and
   great !

Sit throned on either ocean and watch thy sons increase,

And keep the seas for freedom and hold the lands for
   peace !

Thy fleets shall bear the harvest from all thy daughter-
   lands,

And o'er thy blue sea-highways the continents join
   hands.

But should some new intruder rise to bind the ocean's
   bride,

Should once thy wave-dominion be questioned or
    denied,
Then rouse thee from thy happy dream, go forth and
    be again
The England of our hero-sires who broke the might
    of Spain.

THOBAL.

THERE was bloody work in the border hills, as it drew
    to Easter-tide,
And the flag that waved for England was humbled
    there in its pride,

They were grim familiar tidings, those few dark words
    of doom,
For the wide outposts of Empire are marked by the
    lonely tomb;—

There was no new phase in the story, but another
    page writ red,
The ambush laid, and the few too few, and the roll of
    English dead!

And we doubted not of the duty done, we were sure
    they had died like men,
And we knew that the flag of England would float on
    its mast again.

But it chanced there were thirty Ghoorkas who were
   marching on their way,
With fifty more of the Burman folk that have learned
   the word "obey,"

When the scouts brought in the tidings, and the blood
   lust made them mad,
These eighty men of the loyal folk led on by an
   English lad.

And he did not wait nor waver, he took no count of
   the odds.
For he knew that he stood for England in the face of
   the painted gods ;

Though the hills poured down their thousands, if the
   sturdy pluck held true,
He would stand his ground and show them what an
   English lad could do.

So a week went by in silence, and at last the message
   came,
And the eighty men of Thobal had saved the English
   name.

Then speak, oh mother island, for was it not well
    done ?

Be proud of thy step-children, and proudest of thy
    son !

Once more the world has seen it, far under alien
    skies,

The beating heart of England is where the old flag
    flies.

What though they deem thou sleepest, and smile to see
    thee range,

And follow wandering voices on many a wind of
    change ;

What though men say thy gospel is the counter and
    the till,

The boys we send to the far world's end have the
    heart of the lion still ;

The heart of Richard Grenville when he fought with
    the fifty-three,

As he bled to death in the battered hull that was lost
    in the Spanish sea ;

The heart of Walter Raleigh, and the heart of Francis
    Drake,
The heart of all the heroes who have lived for
    England's sake ;

The heart of those who ventured on many a hopeless
    quest,
Till their dear divine unreason had joined the east
    and west.

You boys that man the warships that are the ocean
    queens,
Come back and tell your fathers what that name
    of England means.

Round all the world's wide girdle, in Asia's dark
    defiles,
In the yellow sands of torrid lands, in tempest-
    sundered isles,

O'er many a lonely station the trebled crosses
    wave,
For justice to the weaker, and for freedom to the
    slave !

God send her rulers wisdom,—the task to tame the
    lands,
The peril path of Empire is safe in these young
    hands.

Though the air be filled with strange new sound, and
    perplexed with doubtful creeds,
The boys we send to the far world's end still know
    what England needs.

THE BURIAL OF DRAKE.

In the roads off Nombre Dios
  The last ship lay of ten,
Against a sullen sunset rose
  The ridge of Darien :

For ten that sailed from Plymouth
  Shall one sail home again,
For storm and death and sickness
  Have done the work of Spain.

So, grave and heavy-hearted,
  We watched the setting sun,
For we must leave untenanted
  The islands that we won.

The sky was red and angry,
  The heaving waves were red,
And in his shotted hammock lay
  Our great sea-captain dead.

Defeat nor failure had not cowed
 The will they could not break,
But years and toil and fever
 Had wrought on England's Drake.

His men stood ringed about him,
 And every head was bowed,
St. George's red-cross banner
 Shall be his ocean shroud.

His soul was wide as ocean
 And boundless as the breeze,
He left us for inheritance
 The freedom of the seas.

A faithful servant, serving man,
 He served his Maker best,
And as his path was on the waves,
 The waves shall guard his rest.

We said a brief prayer o'er him,
 And gave him to the deep,
Far off by Nombre Dios
 The billows rock his sleep.

And the clouds of heaven opened
For the tropic rain to fall,
The last day gleam went under,
And darkness spread his pall.

THE PASSING OF ODIN.

(*The Cradle of the Race.*)

THIS song was borne on the north wind's wings, a grim
   old riddle of rhyme,
From the edge of the outer silence, a song of the
   night of time—

A song unsung in the runes of old, for bards save
   him there were none,
In the day of the passing of Odin, when his work in
   the world was done.

He had led his folk from a ravished land, a nation
   haggard and few,
With age-long battle and wandering years, to a shore
   that no man knew ;

Where fenced by the shield of winter, and lit by a
   frosty moon,
The passion of earth had left untried the land of the
   sunless noon :

And there he had stayed his people, the rocks of
 the fiords for home,
Braced strong by the battle of nature, and stern as the
 wind and the foam.

So they tamed the wild for their portion, they slew the
 seal in the wave,
They fought the wolf in his mountain lair, and they
 tracked the bear to his cave ;

While he built them ships, and he forged them swords,
 and there by the misty tide
In the simple shadow of Odin's law they grew and
 they multiplied ;

And the light came back to their hungry eyes, their
 lips were retuned to mirth,
And they prospered there in the sea-born world, as
 the years rolled over the earth.

Now it fell at the death of autumn, when the suns
 hung low in the skies,
That his word went forth to the people, and they came
 to the Wise of the Wise.

The clouds were big with the early snow and the bode
    of a storm to be,
And he led them down when the short day died to
    the edge of the throbbing sea :

A keen wind blew from the mountain land, it howled
    through the clefts and caves,
It groaned in the fir, and it sighed in the birch, and
    it died with a wail in the waves ;

And he took his stand in the dragon ship, on the deck
    by the pine-stem mast,
While it strained on the twisted hawser, and shook in
    the seaward blast;

But the folk drew round in a circle, the flickering
    torch struck red
On their strong lithe limbs, on the sea-blue eyes, on
    the fur-capped fair-haired head :

Then over the wave and wind at war his voice rose
    steady and strong,
Rose winged with a passion of earnest to the lilt of a
    saga-song.—

" It has come, it has come, my people, with the first
 few flakes of the snow,
The snow of the seventy winters, and the day that I
 must go !

" Too long, too long, oh my people, the souls of my
 swordsmen wait
Till I come to my home in Asgard, where they sit by
 the waiting-gate :

" The task is done and the years are told I may bide
 in the worldly ways,
And the laws are all recorded to last till the end of
 days.

" But before I am gone, my people, give ear to the
 word of sooth,
And treasure it up for the after-time if ever I told you
 truth !

" The rocks shall be your cradle, ye shall ride unscared
 on the waves,
The sword shall be your language, and the winds shall
 be your slaves,

"Till the sons of your sons grow round you like the
   leaves of the forest tree,
Like the stars of the night in number, like the shingles
   under the sea.

"Till the land grows straight for the tale of them,—
   then the sign is, ye shall know,
When they draw the sword on each other, and hunger
   comes with the snow.

"Lo, I see far down in the future three blood-red
   ships of the North,
With the men and the maids of my people put out
   from the open forth;

"Three ships that the wind shall sever, borne each to
   a different strand,
One to the east, and one to the west, and one to the
   middle-land.

"The tide of their might shall urge them, as the tide
   sweeps up the fiord
They shall shriek my name for a battle-cry, and shall
   write my name on the sword;

" For the lust of battle is on them, the sea's blue light
  in their eyes,
As the blast of the snow-wind bears them away to the
  gentler skies,

" There shall no man stand before them, when they
  march in the might of strength,
And earth shall shudder and know them through the
  whole of her breadth and length ;

" Till for every rood of the land we lost she shall
  yield them a hundred-fold :
For every head that was humbled once shall be ten
  heads crowned with gold.

" The south shall bow before them, and the west
  acclaim them lords,
The east shall quake at the painted ships and the men
  of the wintry fiords ;

" They shall sway undreamed dominions by the salt of
  an unknown wave,
And every shore that the ocean wets be the portion of
  my brave.

"Lo, this is the sooth of Odin, and the rest is dark
to show,

For the Norns spin on in silence, but the after-time
shall know.

"And now, farewell, oh my people, keep all my words
in your heart,

For the seventy years are numbered, and the time has
come to part;

"Farewell, for the wind blows seaward, and the snow-
flakes fret and fall,

In the day foredoomed by the waiting-gate I will hear
my children call."

And when he had ended speaking, he clutched at his
battle brand

And waved it round in the torchlight, for the might
was still in his hand,

And swift through the lungs and breast-bone he drave
it with might and main,

And snatched it forth with a mystic cry to ravin it
through again;

While an awe fell over the people as they stared with
  abated breath,
For the weird of words, and the wound he made, and
  the riddle of life in death.

So nine times gashed he his breast and side, and every
  wound was a span,
And the first, or the last, or the least of them had been
  death to a common man ;

But erect stood he till the thrice-third stroke, then he
  left the brand in his side,
And slipped the knot of the gathered sail as he fell on
  the deck and died :

While a wail went up from a thousand lips, that hung
  in the mountain cleft,
And shuddered away in the echoes, the wail of his
  folk bereft ;

While ever the wave grew wilder, and ever the wind
  more loud,
And the white snow-flakes came swirling, the stars
  went out in the cloud ;

While the stout ship strained at the twisted hemp, till
    it snapped like a thread in the blast,
And away with a bound in the night and storm the
    shadow of Odin passed.

MISCELLANEOUS POEMS.

MISCELLANEOUS POEMS.

TO BEATRICE.

Incomminciai: Madonna, mia bisogna
Voi conoscete, e ciò ch'adessa è buono.
Purg. xxxiii.

ANGEL and blessed spirit ! where thou art
In the far silence, for a little while
Turn back thine eyes upon our darkling sphere,
Forego the glory for a little while,
And see and hear and say if I do well.

Angel and blessed spirit ! lo, thine eyes
Are opened, seeing all things through and through.
Was not the longing of my whole life drawn
To one star's light so peerless and so pure
It might not linger with the world too long ?

K

And in that star the worshipped and unwon
I had my earthly gladness, unallured
By meaner lusts and longings, till it passed
Back to the radiance by whose grace it grew
Beyond the gulf that severs life and death.

Yet, if his star went down behind the sea
And left the dark night poorer, shall he steer
Starless and guideless on a dreary deep,
Forego all solace for one star's eclipse,
Who needs must traverse the great wave of time ?

Angel and blessed spirit ! where thou art
Safe in the rose's heart of Paradise,
None thirsts for love or kinship any more,
But ever heart in heart as hand in hand
The saints are sistered in a loftier love.

But we, whose path is still to run below
By darker roads and stormy,—dost thou say
Relenting to the human need ?—must make
Best use of all earth's uses, and hold fast
What help we may of laughter and of love.

I knew a summit that I might not climb,
A height too holy for a heart like mine,
Unreached indeed, but not unreachable,
An earthly linked to an ideal love,
A mountain tapering to a star.

Angel and blessed spirit ! bid me drink
The cup of life, and for the rest trust God,
That he who showed the blossom ere it blew
Keeps somewhere still the promised fruit, no less
That other leaves presumed upon the bough.

For there is that within me cries aloud,
For joy, for love, resents its solitude ;
The live man's blood within me will not freeze
Into the cold ideal, such excess
Of life He gave, who gives as best him seems.

How should I do without the human hope
Who have one life to venture, how renounce
The children's laughter and the clinging hands
The centred sympathy that heals a hurt,
The little things that make the great things prized ?

Oh you that taught the possible of God,
The soul's love soaring out of earthly reach,
Suffer the heart's love, that I may not lose
All in a vain high longing, and go down
With life's life frozen from its debt and due!

So, since I take this jewel to my heart,
To fill the longing that I would not lack,
Bless thou the bond, and still, so blessing be,
Because my dream was higher than my hope,
An inspiration, and perchance a prayer.

1889.

HERBSTGEFÜHL.

You are his, his only, all through and through,
　　And the rest was long ago,—
There is nothing done that I would undo,
　　Who believe you happy so.

Your years are full, there is no beyond,
　　You drift on a gentle stream,
And the children's eyes are a better bond
　　Than the old uneasy dream.

But it may be at times when the sun goes down
　　In a certain dip to the west,
In the autumn time, when the fields are brown,
　　When the wind goes through the nest,

When the year is tired of its green display,
　　One wandering thought may be,—
When the heart is tuned to the autumn grey,—
　　Goes over the world to me ;

And I think you muse, for a moment's space,—
    Had it all been otherwise,
Till a tender thought for a vanished face
    Comes back on the dreaming eyes ;

And those are my moments, mine,—in the hush
    I win you a little while,
And now and again in the rosy blush
    I have seen the olden smile.

Where I walk alone in the mist and doubt,
    It was kind, dear heart, to dare
In the autumn eve, in the world without,
    To come and see how I fare ;

It was kind, dear heart, it was worthy of you,
    When the lights burn bright within !
For what has a face like yours to do
    With trouble and life and sin !

Turn back, sweet face, from the window-ledge,
    Turn back, for the children call.---
The sun goes down on the ocean's edge,
    And once more the shadows fall.

INVOCATION.

Come down to the spirit garden
    That I made in my soul for you !
By the path where the ghostly roses
    Are wet with the moony dew.

Step over the sand of silver,
    Close down to the waveless sea !—
Not yet, not yet is the white sail set
    Of the ship that makes us free.

But I know you know I am waiting
    With my face to the moonlit sea,
And your eyes are wan, for the soul is gone
    To walk on the sands with me.

So far you are, yet by moon and star
    I may stand with your hand in mine,
When none is aware of our meeting,
    And the silence gives no sign,

For it needs not a word or a whisper

When the voice is a beating heart, —

And hand in hand on the ghostly sand

We smile at the seas that part.

THE PRINCESS AT THE WINDOW.

(*A Picture.*)

1790.

I WISH just once I could lay aside
   These robes, run down on my little feet
Through the palace gate, where the roads divide,
   Quite unobserved to the crowded street,
Where the plain folk walk and the world is wide.

I wonder how much of their life I miss,—
   I think I never was quite a child,
As the children are that they bring to kiss ;
   I wonder if I shall grow reconciled
To a life that is ever and only this.

Just seventeen, when they bade me wed !
   My grave young Duke who has won the prize,
He is brave and honest, and all is said—
   But if this is the meaning of love, what lies
Are all the poems I ever read !

I have never in all my years run free
   In the dear green woods, on the mountain side;
I never have been alone with the sea,—
   There was only one day, when my mother died,
That I had my way, and they let me be.

But ever the bows and the bending dames !
   And my ladies who wait in the ante-room,
Where the grim forefathers stare from their frames,
   And the glitter of light is full of gloom,
And the pomp and the pride of it only names.

When I walk to-night in the palace show,
   And the world on tip-toe crowds to see,
I shall muse to myself,—could you only know,
   I think you need none of you envy me,—
As I watch the faces along the row.

My father the king, with his stately grace,
   Will bend from the step of the throne above
To print a kiss on the upturned face;
   And the people will stare at the royal love,
And feel us near to their common-place.

But I shall sit in the right-hand seat,
 And smile my welcome and play my part,
And words will mingle and eyes will meet,
 But I shall not get near one human heart
To be quite quite sure of its beat.

Just now we drove through the public square,
 There was one that played on a harp, and one,
A sweet young child with the wind in her hair,
 And she sang as a bird sings out in the sun,
While the crowd forsook her for us to stare.

And I thought to myself as I heard her sing,
 How never for her can the days be long,
Do the hours drag with a trailing wihg,
 Though the feet be weary and sad the song,—
And I almost envied that homeless thing.

Oh you with the hate in your heart grown blind,
 Who would strike us down from our place above,
I wish you could read what I have in my mind,
 And how hungry I am for a little love
And the human touch with my kind!

FOR A GRAVE.

PANSIES first and violets blue,
While our thought is full of you,
While they name you soft and low,
Lest the heart should overflow.

Roses in a little while,
When we learn again to smile,
When our sorrow finds relief
In the sympathy of grief.

Lilies last in later years,
After time has dried our tears,
Such as brother Lippo paints
In the hands of happy saints.

A PARTING.

THE light was dim, and she and I
Alone as in the days gone by;
The firelight played about her hair,
And from the old familiar chair
I watched her sitting at my feet;—
The rain was dripping in the street.

" Now let your hand rest in my hand,
The quicker so to understand,
And let your eyes look through and through
These eyes that look their last on you,—
And tell me if I fail in aught
To read the fashion of your thought.

" Between the summer and the spring
Young birds begin to feel the wing,
And when the summer's in the sky
The little wings are strong to fly:—
With you 'tis hardly summer yet,
I was at summer ere we met.

" Your lot was cast in happy lines,
You had the instinct which divines
The music of the world, the mirth
Such eager hearts require of earth,
The ready tears for human things,
The dream, the hope, the want of wings.

" And yet your years were slow to find
The sunward path your soul divined ;
A tide of life was surging round,
Whose voice was but an empty sound,
And these would hardly realize
The vision of your dreaming eyes.

" And then I chanced to come your way,
To please some destiny at play;
And seemed like one who had the key
To dreamlands you had longed to see ;
You wanted what I had to give,
You longed to know, to feel, to live.

" So I became a whole year long
The echo of your morning song ;

With me you dipped in hidden lore
Of sage and singer gone before,
And, as a child, so hand in hand
I led you into fairyland.

" I told you all I hoped of men,
 The task of heroes now, and then,
While step by step, as poets can,
I built you the ideal man,
And, building, taught you first to see
How far away he was from me."

And there I stopped a moment's space
And looked into the wistful face,
And something like a little sigh
Was all she gave me for reply ;—
She did not draw away her hand,
I could not choose but understand.

" Child, what you most esteemed in me
Was never there in due degree ;
It was the faith in you constrained,
And either gave what either gained ;
Since you believed me pure and true,
I tried to be so, dear, for you.

" But now that love has found you out,
Your heart is tortured with a doubt ;
Because at last you've learned to reach
A secret that I did not teach,
You tremble lest perchance you guess
The reason of my faithfulness.

" And so, because I go to-day
To lands and peoples far away,
And years might pass in doubt and pain
Before our footsteps meet again,
I came back to acquit you, dear,
Of any shade of doubt or fear :

" Because I found a kindred soul,
A straining for a common goal,
It was my joy to taste with you
Those heather scents and mountain dew,
To give the best I had to give,
And learn the better how to live :

" Another hand will guide you now,—
But if you reach our mountain brow,

Still keep a corner in your mind

For one who, maybe, lags behind,

Who found it hard indeed to part,

But, still could leave you, whole of heart."

She rose, and bent her brow to kiss,

And there I scaled the truth of this,—

One last look more,—she turned and smiled,

It was the woman, not the child ;—

The rain was falling fast outside :

God will forgive me if I lied !

1889.

L

NOTES.

NOTES.

Page 19.—THERMOPYLÆ.

The pass of Thermopylæ, in the strict sense of the word, exists no longer. The whole configuration of the land has changed. The alluvial deposits of the Spercheius, which enters the Maliac gulf from the valley dividing Oeta from Othrys, have created a marshy plain of several square miles in extent, where once the sea came up in shallows to the precipitous mountain side, leaving only the narrow road, some fifty feet in breadth, across which ran the wall whence the Greeks sallied out for the first two days' battle. The sulphur springs, which gave the place its name, have also evidently changed their course repeatedly, and their spreading waters have covered with a thick and ever-increasing saline deposit the exact spot where the fighting took place. It is still a wild and desolate scene. Crane and heron flap their dusky wings over miles of waving rushes between the rock wall and the sea; the peaks of Callidromus break the blue sky, whence the fierce sun burns down on the yellow crystal-crusted floor, over which the shadows of the poising eagles pass. The only sign of human habitation is a ruined mill, and the spirit of solitude seems to haunt the place.—*From my Journal in Greece.*

Page 23.—Delos.

The lesser Delos, the sacred island, is a granite rock rising to a considerable elevation in the central height of Cynthus, which gave its name to the two children of Latona. In the distance, it appeared bare and treeless ; but as we approached, we discovered that it was a very isle of flowers—everywhere between the granite boulders were innumerable marigolds and scarlet poppies. Save for the solitary guardian in his hut among the ruins, the island has no regular inhabitants, but a few shepherds from the neighbouring Mykonos come over with their flocks from time to time to pasture and to reap the scanty harvest. . . . . Half-way up the slope of Cynthus stands the grotto, or to be more exact, the primitive rock temple of the Sun God, probably the oldest place of worship in Greece. Before it lies a wilderness of ruin, the bases and substructions of what must have formed as grand a group of buildings as the world could show : fallen columns, broken cornices, masses of wrought and carven stones piled one upon the other in formless, hopeless confusion. . . . . The great temple of Apollo still admits of identification, the rest of little more than conjecture.—

From my Journal in Greece.

Page 33.—Tænaron.

"A race as wild as nature where they dwell."

The Mainotes who occupy the rocky promontory, which is in reality a prolongation of the range of Taygetus, terminating in Cape Matapan, boast that in all the vicissitudes through which the Morea has passed they alone have never submitted to a foreign domination. They claim to be the descendants of the Spartans of old, and are most probably the direct descendants of the Periœci of Lakonia, who occupied the poorer lands round the coasts, and who were by origin Hellenes, settled there before the Dorian invasion. They are quite different in physical type from their neighbours, and their language abounds in Doricisms, and is closely akin to that spoken by the Dorian Sphakiotes in the mountains of Crete.

It is certain that the various invaders of the Peloponnese have always endeavoured to conciliate the dwellers in the wild promontory, whose pathless mountains and barren plateau would have been very difficult to occupy ; but, nevertheless, they have always been the first to rise against the foreigner. Their land is the bleakest and poorest conceivable, and not calculated to tempt the invader. Nevertheless, they are passionately attached to it, and ever ready to fight in its behalf. Their villages are mere nests of towers loopholed for defence ; and the vendetta exists between family and family, between village and village, and among them a greater number of old - world usages are preserved than anywhere else in Greece. They still enjoy exceptional privileges at the hands of the government, such as immunity from taxation, which it would be useless to attempt to collect, and hitherto comparatively few foreigners have visited their desolate but romantic home. —

From my Journal in Greece.

Page 46.—TANAGRA.

Of Korinna's poetry no fragment survives ; and all that is known of her is drawn from the account Pausanias has given of his visit to Tanagra. There he saw her portrait, the beauty of which struck him so much that he suggests it was perhaps her grace and charm which won the Theban judges to accord her the prize in the contest of song over their own immortal Pindar. In a little shed in a neighbouring village are a few fragments of sculptured stone and a number of clay coffins from the site of Tanagra. Among them is a gravestone which bears Korinna's name.

Page 49.—The Song of the Klepht.

The popular poetry of Greece is very comprehensive and rich, and among its most interesting features are the so-called Klephtic ballads, celebrating the exploits of those outlawed mountaineers who throughout the Turkish domination kept the spirit of freedom alive in their rocky fastnesses, whence they maintained an unceasing desultory warfare with the invader. The origin and history of these marauding bands is still somewhat obscure; but it would appear that while those of the Greek peasantry who submitted to the Mussulman yoke were allowed considerable liberties, and permitted to form a sort of irregular militia, known as the *Armatoli*, for the defence of privileges originally conceded, others, rejecting all overtures of the conqueror, took to the mountains, and formed themselves into armed bands, carrying on a guerilla warfare against the Turkish governors, and making raids upon the new settlers, not always sparing those of their countrymen who had submitted to the foreigner. These men were known by the appellation of *Klephts*, a name which, signifying originally *robber*, was ere long regarded as a title of distinction. Later, when the *Armatoli* came into conflict with the Mussulman militia, the distinction between them and the Klephts practically passed away, and it was from their ranks that the foremost fighters in the Hellenic uprising were drawn. The ballads in which their exploits were told were sung by blind beggars at the village fairs at the close of the last and the commencement of the present century, and thus these men of the mountain, whose lives were passed entirely in the open air, moving from range to range where plunder or revenge allured them, became the darling heroes of the popular imagination, which credited them with almost fabulous powers of strength and endurance.

The Klephts of the continent and the corsairs of the islands and the coasts were the protest of liberty against a foreign domination, and the voice of the humbler people, glorying in nobilities which other lands and times might question, has painted them with sympathetic indulgence, perhaps not wholly as they were, but rather as they would have had them be. Their indifference to hardships, pain, and death, their loyalty of comradeship, their physical courage, were beyond all question, and the folk-ballads in which their names are preserved are the note of ideality, rising above the actual brutalities and bloodshed which characterized an era of struggle and rebellion. A full account of the Klephts and Klephtic songs may be found in my "Customs and Lore of Modern Greece."

The poem included in this volume is not a translation. It embodies the expression of one or two snatches of folk-song in an attempt to convey the savage spirit and rugged picturesqueness of the popular muse of Greece a hundred years ago.

Liméri, the name given to the mountain *rendezvous* of the Klephts where they spent the day, setting forth on their raids rather on moonless and cloudy nights in order to escape observation. The etymology of the word is ὅλη ἡμέρα = *the whole day*. In such meeting-places on the summits of well-nigh unscalable rocks they would keep their stores of ammunition hidden in caves or rock-fissures, and thither they would bring their plunder and camp secure, spending the day in gymnastic exercises, in practising their aim, or in singing to the sound of a rude mandoline known as the lyra.

Liápids.—The Liápids are a tribe of Mussulman Albanians. A great number of them took service under Ali, the notorious Pacha of Jannina, and the name was applied by the Greeks and Christian Albanians as a term of contempt to the Mussulman militia generally.

Page 53.—ZALONGOS.

There is no more romantic page in history than that which tells the story of the little mountain commonwealth of Suli, which for so many years defied the authority and repulsed the trained armies of the notorious Ali Pacha of Jannina. The origin of the Suliotes is somewhat obscure, though a chronicler has professed to trace their history back into the 17th century. The principal families undoubtedly derived their origin from different districts, and although their language was Greek, they seem to have consisted chiefly of Christian Albanians, with a smaller admixture of Greeks, who, flying before the oppression of the Moslem invader, had taken refuge in the almost inaccessible mountains of Chimari, where they established a patriarchal community, governed by the heads of their families or clans, which were known as *pharas.* They had neither laws nor law-courts, but the heads of the families acted as arbiters in all disputes, and met in a council, the matter for whose deliberations was almost exclusively war.

At the time when they became conspicuous in history they possessed four villages in the mountain of Suli, and seven in the plain, the Tetrachorion and the Heptachorion. At one time they also controlled between fifty and sixty subject villages, which were, however, abandoned to their fate in war. The inhabitants of the seven lower villages, on the other hand, being regarded as genuine Suliotes, were allowed, on the commencement of hostilities, to retire into the mountain, which is approached by one of the wildest and deepest defiles in all these rugged ranges. In places the way is only practicable on foot along a perilous ledge, high up the vertical side of the mountain of Suli, whence far below, in the gloom of the chasm, the Acheron may be seen falling in cascades over the rocks, but silently, owing to the depth and distance.

The total number of the mountain community never exceeded 5,000 souls, and they could not put more than 1,500 fighting men into the field ; and yet with this little force they kept the armies of Ali at bay for a number of years, and inflicted several signal defeats on his trained Albanian troops. They had brought the tactics of the Klephtic warfare to perfection ; from childhood they were trained marksmen, and moved over their wild mountains with the agility of a chamois. The women often fought beside the men, and the many folk-songs which record the exploits of Suli are full of acts of heroism performed by the wives and mothers of the mountaineers. Concealed among the scrub, or hidden behind boulders of rock, they fought with comparative impunity, and so quick was their eye, that it is said they could fire with deadly effect by night at the flash of their enemies' guns. At the time when Ali, appointed " warden of the passes," was attempting to put down the irregular bands which infested the Pindus, and to consolidate his power in north-western Greece, the Suliotes were led by an ascetic priest or monk, Samuel, who believed himself to be, and was certainly regarded by the mountaineers as an inspired prophet. By his direction they built the fortress of Kiunghi, in the inmost recesses of their mountain, as a store-house for their ammunition and material. It was here in the church that the powder stores were gathered, to which Samuel set fire, immolating himself among the ruins at the close of their eventful story, rather than surrender, to the emissaries of Ali, the keys with which he had been entrusted.

Towards the close of the last century an expedition upon a large scale was led by Ali in person, to reduce the defiant Suliotes to subjection. But his 15,000 picked Albanians were drawn on by the tactics of the mountaineers far into the rocky defiles, and at a given moment attacked by the Suliote women in front, and simultaneously by an ambush of the men under

Bótzaris and Lambros Tzavellas in flank and rear. A wild panic
ensued ; Ali himself fled in terror back to Jannina, and was
forced to sue for peace, and yield important concessions. Eight
years later the unequal struggle began again. Ali had recourse
to every art of treachery and corruption to break up the solidarity
of the little commonwealth, and succeeded in gaining over one
or two of the more important families. His son Veli, isolating
their various strongholds, and attacking them in overwhelming
numbers, succeeded in overpowing them one by one after a
desperate resistance, under the leadership of the young Photos,
son of Lambros Tzavellas. The survivors, attacked once more
when marching into neutral territory under the capitulation they
had forced Ali to agree to, retired to fight a last battle on the
heights of Zalongos. It was then that the episode occurred
which forms the subject of this poem.

Kiapha, Avarikos, Samoniva, and *Kako-Suli* formed the
Tetrachorion, to which the fortress of *Kiunghi* was added later.

Liápids—see note to the " Song of the Klepht."

The Pharas of the Mountain, the clans or families—see
above.

To sit perchance at Byron's door.—In the heroic story of
Misolonghi, another Bótzaris and another Tzavellas will long be
remembered. The name of Suliote was still a terror when
Byron came for the last time to Greece, and the glorious death
of Marco Bótzaris at Karpenisi recalled to interest the extra-
ordinary exploits of his countrymen some twenty years before.

Page 67.—FOLK-SONGS.

Charos.—Among the most curious survivals of ancient myth is
the reappearance of the ferryman of Styx as the angel of death,
or rather as the personification of an inexorable law of nature.

The identification of Charon with Thanatos occurs in classical authors more than once; and as in Homer the father and fountain of sacred myth, the boatmen of hell is unknown, it is not impossible that the popular superstition has preserved the direct inheritance of a still older and less complex idea. He is pictured in the folk-poetry as an old man of sorrowful face, immovable to prayer, crafty and jealous, taking swift vengeance on those who defy his power, and glory unduly in their youth and strength. Sometimes he is represented as the direct emissary of the Deity, but he dwells and controls the dead in that dark undefined land so often alluded to in the popular poetry, where the souls of the departed regret the sun and the trees and the fountains, that pagan land of nothingness which here still seems to appeal to the popular mind more powerfully than the promise of heaven or the menace of hell. This subject, with the various aspects of the Charos myth as it exists to-day, is treated exhaustively in my "Customs and Lore of Modern Greece,' chap. iv.

Page 72.—Akrotiri of Crete.

This barren mountainous peninsula forms one side of Suda Bay.

Page 80.—Pentelikon.

The Pentelic mountain was so called from the Attic deme of Pentele, in which it was included. The ancients also spoke of it under the name of Brilettus. On its slopes is the monastery of Mendeli, a hospitable refuge in the great heats of summer.

The crescent plain.—Marathon.

Page 92.—A Ballad of the Armada.

This poem, which was written on the occasion of the Ter-centenary, is far from being put forward in emulation of Lord Macaulay's famous fragment. It is rather meant as a continuation of what he unfortunately left uncompleted, and deals with the aspect of things at sea, whereas his poem only tells of what took place on shore.

Page 129.—To Beatrice.

" And since I take this *jewel* to my heart."—Gemma Donati.

Henderson & Spalding, Limited, Printers, 3 & 5, Marylebone Lane, W.